THE WITCH'S DOG AND
THE FLYING CARPET

Frank Rodgers has written and illustrated a wide range of books for children: picture books, story books, how-to-draw books and a novel for teenagers. His work for Puffin includes the highly popular *Intergalactic Kitchen* series and the picture books *The Bunk-Bed Bus* and *The Pirate and the Pig*, as well as the best-selling *Witch's Dog* titles. He was an art teacher for a number of years before becoming an author and illustrator. He lives in Glasgow with his wife and two children.

Frank Rodgers
The Witch's Dog and the Flying Carpet

PUFFIN BOOKS

PUFFIN BOOKS

Published by the Penguin Group
Penguin Books Ltd, 27 Wrights Lane, London W8 5TZ, England
Penguin Putnam Inc., 375 Hudson Street, New York, New York 10014, USA
Penguin Books Australia Ltd, Ringwood, Victoria, Australia
Penguin Books Canada Ltd, 10 Alcorn Avenue, Toronto, Ontario, Canada M4V 3B2
Penguin Books India (P) Ltd, 11 Community Centre, Panchsheel Park,
New Delhi – 110 017, India
Penguin Books (NZ) Ltd, Cnr Rosedale and Airborne Roads, Albany,
Auckland, New Zealand
Penguin Books (South Africa) (Pty) Ltd, 5 Watkins Street, Denver Ext 4,
Johannesburg 2094, South Africa

On the World Wide Web at: www.penguin.com

Penguin Books Ltd, Registered Offices: Harmondsworth, Middlesex, England

First published 2001
1 3 5 7 9 10 8 6 4 2

Printed in Hong Kong by Midas Printing Ltd

British Library Cataloguing in Publication Data
A CIP catalogue record for this book is available from the British Library

ISBN 0–141–31221–1

Wilf, the Witch's Dog, stared
glumly at his plant.
There were no flowers on it.

1

"I don't think this plant is growing properly, Weenie," he called. "We're making a garden at school and everyone is bringing something for it. I won't have anything."

Weenie popped her head round the door. "I'll have a look in a moment, Wilf," she said. "I'm busy cleaning the spare room.

My granny and grandpa are coming to visit."

"Are they?" said Wilf. "Then I'll help you."

He put down the flowerpot and joined Weenie.

"What can I do?" he asked.

Weenie pointed to a rolled-up carpet in the cupboard.

"You could give that a shake," she said. "It's an old favourite of mine and it would look nice by the fireside."

Wilf took the carpet outside and
unrolled it.

Taking hold of one end, he gave it a
good shake.
A cloud of dust puffed out just as
Wilf's friends, Harry, Bertie
and Streaky,
arrived.

Streaky walked straight into the
dust cloud.
"Achoo!"
he sneezed ...

... and shot backwards into the air.
"What a sneeze!"
said Bertie.

But Streaky
didn't stop
shooting
backwards ...

... he kept going. He went higher
and higher and faster and faster.
"Help!" he shouted.
"I like going fast,
but not like this!"

"If he keeps
going, he'll land
on the moon!"
cried Harry.

"Wilf, do something!"

Wilf leaped forward.
"Give me your scarf, Harry!" he
cried.

Wilf handed one
end to Bertie.
"Hold on to this
as tightly as
you can," he
said.

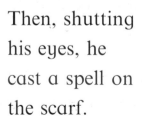

Then, shutting
his eyes, he
cast a spell on
the scarf.

"Whoa!" said Bertie,
as the scarf wriggled in
his hands as if
it were a
snake.

Suddenly ...

WHOOOOOSH!

The scarf stretched upwards like a
banner in the wind.

9

It streamed out longer and
longer into the sky
until it reached
Streaky.

He caught the end and held on
tightly.

Streaky came to a sudden stop.

Bertie was
nearly pulled off
his feet, but he
was strong and
didn't let go.

Streaky tied the scarf firmly round
his waist.
"Heave!" shouted
Bertie and quickly pulled
Streaky back down to
the garden.

"What's going on?"
cried Weenie,
rushing out.

Wilf explained about the dust from the carpet.

"Oh dear," said Weenie, "I remember now. I once tried to make that into a flying carpet. I used magic dust. There must have been some left on it."

"There's still some left on me," said Streaky, bobbing in the air like a balloon.

"Sorry, Streaky," said Weenie. Quickly, she cast a spell. In no time Streaky and the scarf came back to normal.

Weenie looked at the carpet.
"The moths have been eating it,"
she said.

"It's full of
holes."

"Can I try and fix it, Weenie?" said
Wilf.

"I could
practise my
mending
spell."

14

"Good idea," Weenie replied.
Wilf laid the carpet on the ground.
Then he shut his eyes and
concentrated hard.

The spell shot
out ...

But the spell didn't mend the holes.
Instead, it filled them in with real
flowers!

16

"Ha!" said Harry with a laugh.
"You've made a carpet of flowers,
Wilf!"
Wilf grinned.
"I could bring it to
school tomorrow,"
he said.

"I didn't really want to use magic. I
hope the head teacher won't mind."

The head teacher was delighted.
"I don't mind just this once, Wilf,"
she said. "But anything else has to
be grown without magic."

Everyone admired the carpet of
flowers.
"It's lovely, Wilf," they all said.

Sly Cat and
Tricky Toad
glowered.

They hadn't done anything in the
garden and they were jealous of
Wilf.

"Let's turn his flowers into weeds,"
whispered Sly with a snigger.
"Into weeds," echoed Tricky, and
they both sneaked behind a bush.

When no one was looking they sent
out a spell ...

FLASH!

It crackled over the flowers. But
instead of becoming weeds ...

... they turned into a thick jungle!

"Oh no!" whispered Tricky. "Our
spell went wrong."

"Never mind," hissed Sly with a grin.

"His flowers have
gone. It's still
funny!"

It wasn't funny for long.

Just as everyone was getting over
their surprise, the leaves of the
jungle parted and out stepped ...

... a tiger.
"Ahhh!" Everyone
gasped and backed
away.

The tiger growled nastily and swung
its big ginger head around.

Suddenly it
spotted Sly
and Tricky.

RAAAAAR!

It roared and leaped
towards them.

AAAAAHH!

yelled Sly and Tricky and dodged
behind the bush.

25

"RAAAAR!" roared the tiger again and began to chase them.

Round and round the bush they went.

"AAAAH!" yelled Sly and Tricky.
"RAAAAR!" roared the tiger.

Wilf came to the rescue.
He aimed a vanishing spell at the
tiger and ...

SSSSNAP!

... it disappeared with a pop.

Sly and Tricky didn't notice so they kept running round and round the bush yelling "AAAAH!"

Everyone began to laugh.

Sly and Tricky glanced behind them
and skidded to a halt.

"Very funny!" hissed Sly.

"Yeah, very funny,"
muttered Tricky
and they both
slouched off
angrily.

"Well done, Wilf," said the head teacher. Then her face fell as she looked at the garden.

The jungle had vanished, but the flowers had not returned. Only the old carpet was left.

"I'm afraid we can't have that in the garden," she said.

"You'll have to take it away, Wilf."

Wilf trudged back to Weenie's with the carpet. He didn't notice that Sly and Tricky were following him.

They were still angry because Wilf had made them look foolish.

Weenie sighed when Wilf returned.
"What a shame, Wilf," she said.
"I'm afraid that
neither of us has
had much luck
with that old
thing."

Wilf dropped the carpet on the
ground and sat on it.

"And I've still got to try and grow
something for the school garden,"
he said. "Without magic."

He patted the carpet. "I can't use this again."

Sly and Tricky were hiding behind the hedge sniggering.

"No, you can't use it," Sly hissed, "but we can!"
"Yes ... we can!" echoed Tricky.

Sly and Tricky
chanted a super-
strong spell they
had learned.

ZZZZZ!

A green glow appeared round the
carpet and it gave a little jump.

"What ...?!" cried Wilf
and clutched the
edge of the carpet
as it jumped
again.

"What's happening?"
The carpet bounced underneath him
once more, then ...

ZOOOM

It shot into the
sky with Wilf
still hanging on.

AAAAAAH!

he yelled.

"Oh no!" cried
Weenie.

Sly and Tricky leaned against each
other, shaking with laughter.

"Now that's what I call funny!"
spluttered Sly.
"What I call funny!" repeated
Tricky.

The carpet streaked across the sky.
It swooped like a sledge ...

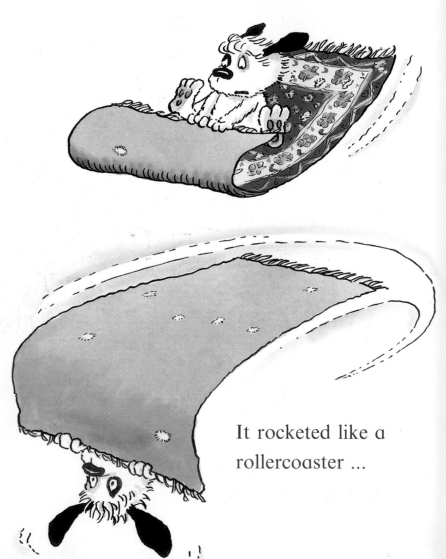

It rocketed like a
rollercoaster ...

It streaked like a jet plane, and all
the time Wilf hung on.

Down in the garden
Weenie was trying all
sorts of magic.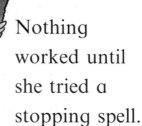

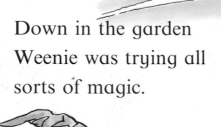

Nothing
worked until
she tried a
stopping spell.

The carpet suddenly screeched to a
halt in mid-air ...

... but Wilf kept going.
"Oops!" he cried
as he skidded
off the carpet.

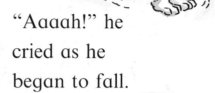

"Aaaah!" he
cried as he
began to fall.

"Oh no!" he gasped
as he tumbled over
and over ... down
and down ...

He tried to think of a floating spell,
but couldn't.
The ground was rushing closer ...
closer ... when suddenly ...

41

WHOOSH!

A broomstick appeared
on either side of him.
It was Weenie's granny and
grandpa. They had arrived for
their visit just in the nick of
time!

"Got you!" they cried.
"Thank you!" gasped Wilf.

42

"Wonderful!" shouted Weenie.

Her granny and grandpa landed
safely with Wilf in Weenie's garden.

At that moment,
Weenie's stopping
spell wore off
and the carpet
dropped out of
the sky.

It almost landed on Sly and Tricky,
but they jumped aside.

As the carpet hit the ground with a
thump, one last little bit of magic
dust puffed up.

Sly and Tricky sneezed together.

AAAACHOO!

They shot
into the
air.

"Heeelp!"
they cried.

Over and over they
tumbled, head over
heels through the
air until they
landed ...

… right in the middle of the school garden's pile of manure.

"Aha!" said the head teacher. "I've been looking for you two.

You haven't done any work in the garden."

Sly and Tricky
squelched out of
the manure, all
smelly and
sticky.

"I'm glad you dropped in," said the
head teacher with a smile. "And as
you've begun to spread the manure,
you can just carry on and finish the
job."

Back in Weenie's garden, her granny and grandpa were catching their breath.

"That was fun!" they said. "We haven't had this much excitement in ages! Phew!"

"You were wonderful!" said Weenie.
"Brilliant!" added Wilf.

He fetched the carpet and Weenie
looked at it. She shook her head.

"That has caused
nothing but
trouble,"
she said.

"Old favourite
or not, it's
going to be
thrown out."

Weenie's granny and grandpa had a lovely visit. After tea in the garden they gave Harry, Bertie and Streaky rides on their broomsticks.

That evening, Weenie threw a party and everyone had a great time.

But next day, when it was time to go, there was a problem.

"Oh dear," groaned Weenie's grandpa. "I'm all sore and stiff. I think I did too much broomstick riding yesterday."

"Me too," said Weenie's granny, rubbing her back.

"I think we're getting too old for broomsticks. It's a shame because we love using them."

51

They shook their heads and sighed.

"No more
broomstick
riding,"
they said.

Weenie frowned.
"How will you get home?" she
asked.

"I've got an idea," said Wilf.
He pointed to the old carpet.

"They could use that,"
he said.

Weenie shook her head.

"I'm afraid that
carpet is useless,
Wilf. It will
never fly
properly."

Wilf grinned and turned to Weenie's
granny and grandpa.
"It will if you attach your
broomsticks to either side of it," he
said.

"You could both sit in the middle
and be nice and comfy."

"That's such a good idea!" said
Weenie's granny and grandpa.

"So it is!" cried Weenie. "My old
favourite would have a use at last!
Wilf, you're a genius!"

Wilf's idea worked perfectly.
"Look! We can put our legs through
the holes," said Weenie's granny.

"It means we won't fall off!" added
Weenie's grandpa with a grin.

56

At last it was time to go. Weenie
said goodbye, and her granny and
grandpa shot into the sky on their
new, broomstick-powered flying
carpet.

"Bye!" they called. "See you soon!"

Back in Weenie's house, Wilf got a surprise.

His plant had started to flower.

"Ah!" said Weenie with a smile. "All you needed was patience, Wilf. You can't hurry nature."

Wilf looked at the new flowers and
smiled in delight.
"Brilliant!" he cried. "I'll be able to
bring my plant to school tomorrow.

I love gardening,"
he said. "Do you
know why,
Weenie?"

Weenie smiled and shook her head.
"Why?" she asked.
"Because," said Wilf ...

"... it works just like magic!"